W9-BMT-402

E   Moreau, Laurent
MOR   Play outside!

DATE DUE			

To Marion and our pretty little Coline

First Published by hélium / Actes Sud © 2018

Library of Congress Control Number: 2019057965

ISBN 9781324015475

W. W. Norton & Company, Inc., 500 Fifth Avenue, New York, N.Y. 10110
www.wwnorton.com

W. W. Norton & Company Ltd., 15 Carlisle Street, London W1D 3BS

1 2 3 4 5 6 7 8 9 0

Oh, no . . . that's enough!
Why don't you two go and . . .

Play Outside!

Laurent Moreau

NORTON YOUNG READERS
An Imprint of W. W. Norton & Company
Independent Publishers Since 1923

You're turning the house upside down.
It's a nice day. Go out in the yard!
You'll find plenty to do. . . .

You can water the garden,

pick flowers and make a bouquet,

lie in the grass and look for shapes in the clouds,

play tag,

hunt for bugs,

run as fast as you can,

and swing from the branches of the trees.

Imagine going on a great adventure,

boarding a sailing ship,

and voyaging to an unknown island.

Feel the wind and sea spray on your face!

Whatever you do, take care.

Remember that nature is fragile!

Go and play outside. By the time you come in you'll have calmed down!

HERE ARE THE ANIMALS THE CHILDREN ENCOUNTERED.
CAN YOU FIND THEM ALL?

Do you know that many animal species around the world are endangered?
But it's not too late to protect them.

The status of the animals in this index is based on the IUCN Red List of Threatened Species (2018).
www.iucnredlist.org

▲▲▲ Critically Endangered
▲▲ Endangered
▲ Vulnerable
■ Near Threatened
● Least Concern
○ Data Deficient

Seashore

DOUBLE-CRESTED CORMORANT
Bird
Europe, North Africa,
North America

NORTHERN GANNET
Bird
Atlantic Ocean

COMMON TURBOT
Fish
Black Sea, Mediterranean
Sea, North Atlantic Ocean,
Pacific Ocean

GREAT CORMORANT
Bird
Africa, Asia, Europe,
North America, Oceania

JELLYFISH
Cnidarian
All marine
environments

ATLANTIC PUFFIN
Bird
Europe, North
America

**COMMON EUROPEAN
SEABASS**
Fish
Europe

PIED AVOCET
Bird
Africa, Asia, Europe

NORTHERN LAPWING
Bird
Asia, Europe, North
Africa

HIGHLAND CATTLE
Mammal
Europe

HIGHLAND PONY
Mammal
Europe

OYSTERCATCHER
Bird
Africa, Europe

HERRING GULL
Bird
Africa, Asia, Europe,
North America
BLACK-HEADED

GULL
Bird
Africa, Asia, Europe,
North America, Oceania

COMMON STARFISH
Starfish
Atlantic Ocean, Mediterranean
Sea, Pacific Ocean

CRAB
Crustacean
Atlantic Ocean,
Mediterranean Sea

GRAY WALLEYE
Fish
Atlantic Ocean, Black Sea,
Mediterranean Sea, Red Sea

BLACKFACE SHEEP
Mammal
Europe

HORSESHOE CRAB
Arthropod
Atlantic Ocean, Indian
Ocean, Pacific Ocean

HARBOR SEAL
Mammal
North Atlantic Ocean,
North Pacific Ocean

Countryside

COW
Mammal
Africa, Americas, Asia,
Europe, Indonesia

DOMESTIC GUINEAFOWL
Bird
Africa, Europe

COYOTE
Mammal
North America

SNOW GOOSE
Bird
Asia, Europe,
North America

RED FOX
Mammal
Africa, Americas,
Asia, Europe

WHITE SPOONBILL
Bird
Africa, Americas,
Asia, Europe

TENCH
Fish
Europe

**DOMESTIC CHICKEN
AND ROOSTER**
Birds
Africa, Americas,
Asia, Europe

BARN SWALLOW
Bird
Africa, Americas,
Asia, Europe

CRANE
Bird
Africa, Americas,
Asia, Europe

DOMESTIC PIG
Mammal
Asia, Europe,
North America

RABBIT
Mammal
Europe, North Africa

EUROPEAN ROBIN
Bird
Asia, Europe,
North Africa

TURTLEDOVE
Bird
Africa, Asia, Europe,
North America

MOLE
Mammal
Asia, Europe,
North America

CHIPMUNK
Mammal
North America

COMMON KINGFISHER
Bird
Europe

OTTER
Mammal
Asia, Europe, Indonesia,
North Africa, North
America, South America

COMMON CATFISH
Fish
Africa, Asia, Europe,
South America

DONKEY
Mammal
Africa, America,
Asia, Europe

RED SWAMP CRAYFISH
Crustacean
Europe

Rivers and Ponds

**SOUTHERN
WATER VOLE**
Mammal
Europe

STORK
Bird
Africa, Asia, Europe

COMMON PERCH
Fish
Europe

DOMESTIC CAT
Mammal
Worldwide

DOMESTIC DOG
Mammal
Worldwide

MUTE SWAN
Bird
Africa, Americas,
Asia, Europe

GREEN FROG
Amphibian
Europe, North America

PIKE
Fish
Europe, North America

GREAT CRESTED GREBE
Bird
Africa, Asia, Europe,
Indonesia

PURPLE HERON
Bird
Africa, Asia, Europe,
South America

REED BUNTING
Bird
Asia, Europe, North Africa,
North America

COMMON GALLINULE
Bird
Africa, Arctic Ocean,
Asia, Europe

BLACK-WINGED STILT
Bird
Africa, Americas, Asia,
Europe, Indonesia

TUFTED DUCK
Bird
Africa, Asia, Europe,
North America

TEAL
Bird
Africa, Asia, Europe,
North America

BLUE EMPEROR DRAGONFLY
Insect
Africa, Asia, Europe

WHISTLING DUCK
Bird
Africa, Asia, Europe,
North America

STARRY BITTERN
Bird
Africa, Asia, Europe

ROACH
Fish
Asia, Australia,
Europe

PEACOCK BUTTERFLY
Insect
Europe

LITTLE BITTERN
Bird
Africa, Asia, Europe,
Indonesia

COMMON CARP
Fish
Asia, Australia, Europe,
North America

EUROPEAN EEL
Fish
Europe, North Africa

AMERICAN BEAVER
Mammal
North America

COMMON LOON
Bird
Europe, North America

Mountains

SNOWFINCH
Bird
Asia, Europe

ROCK PTARMIGAN
Bird
Asia, Europe,
North America

MINNOW
Fish
Europe

BEARDED VULTURE
Bird
Africa, Asia, Europe

ELK
Mammal
Asia, North America

TROUT
Fish
Arctic regions, Europe,
North America

WEASEL
Mammal
Asia, Europe, North
America

GOLDEN EAGLE
Bird
Africa, Asia, Europe,
North America

Mammal
Europe

COUGAR
Mammal
Americas
CHAMOIS

JACKDAW
Bird
Asia, Europe, North
Africa

GRAY WOLF
Mammal
Asia, North America

**EUROPEAN BIGHORN
SHEEP**
Mammal
Europe

ALPINE MARMOT
Mammal
Europe

BEE
Insect
Africa, Asia, Europe,
North America

African
Deserts

DROMEDARY
Mammal
Africa, Middle East

EAST AFRICAN ORYX
Mammal
Africa

EMPEROR SCORPION
Arachnid
Africa

SANDFISH
Reptile
Africa, Middle East

DESERT JERBOA
Mammal
Africa, Middle East

FENNEC FOX
Mammal
Africa

NILE PERCH
Fish
Africa

DAMA GAZELLE
Mammal
Africa

CHEETAH
Mammal
Africa, Middle East

BALD IBIS
Bird
Africa, Middle East

NILE MONITOR
Reptile
Africa

NILE CROCODILE
Reptile
Africa

Savannah

SECRETARYBIRD
Bird
Africa

GIANT GROUND PANGOLIN
Mammal
Africa

PLAINS ZEBRA
Mammal
Africa

LION
Mammal
Africa, Asia, Middle East

YELLOW BABOON
Mammal
Africa

COMMON OSTRICH
Bird
Africa, Australia

WARTHOG
Mammal
Africa

MEERKAT
Mammal
Africa

AFRICAN BUFFALO
Mammal
Africa

SOUTHERN WHITE RHINOCEROS
Mammal
Africa

CROWNED CRANE
Bird
Africa

SPOTTED HYENA
Mammal
Africa

AGAMA
Reptile
Africa

WHITE PELICAN
Bird
Africa, Asia, Europe,
Indonesia, North America

GIRAFFE
Mammal
Africa

MARABOU STORK
Bird
Africa

SACRED IBIS
Bird
Africa, Asia, Europe,
Middle East

RED-CHEEKED CORDONBLEU
Bird
Africa

HIPPOPOTAMUS
Mammal
Africa

IMPALA
Mammal
Africa

WILDEBEEST
Mammal
Africa

OLIVE BABOON
Mammal
Africa

Between River and Jungle

AFRICAN ROCK PYTHON
Reptile
Africa

CHIMPANZEE
Mammal
Africa

BONGO
Mammal
Africa

GIANT TIGERFISH
Fish
Africa

GORILLA
Mammal
Africa

AFRICAN FLYCATCHER
Bird
Africa

LEOPARD
Mammal
Africa, Asia

AFRICAN GREY PARROT
Bird
Africa

FLAMINGO
Bird
Africa, Americas, Asia,
Europe, Indonesia

MANDRILL
Mammal
Africa

AFRICAN CATFISH
Fish
Africa, Middle East

OKAPI
Mammal
Africa

AFRICAN PIKE
Fish
Africa

WESTERN GREEN MAMBA
Reptile
Africa

Asian Forest

GIANT PANDA
Mammal
Asia

KING COBRA
Reptile
Asia, Indonesia

TIGER
Mammal
Asia, Indonesia

WHITE-HANDED GIBBON
Mammal
Asia, Indonesia

DELACOUR'S LANGUR
Mammal
Asia

RED-SHANKED DOUC LANGUR
Mammal
Asia

RED PANDA
Mammal
Asia

WHITE TIGER
Mammal
Asia, Indonesia

ASIAN ELEPHANT
Mammal
Asia, Indonesia

HORNBILL
Bird
Asia

JAPANESE CRESTED IBIS
Bird
Asia

GANGES GHARIAL
Reptile
Indonesia

WALLACE'S FLYING FROG
Amphibian
Indonesia

SIAMESE GIANT CARP
Fish
Southeast Asia

LARGE GLIDER BUTTERFLY
Insect
Asia, Indonesia

BLACK PANTHER
Mammal
Africa, Asia

Pacific Islands and Indian Ocean

KOMODO DRAGON
Reptile
Indonesia

SNAKE-NECKED TURTLE
Reptile
Indonesia

SEA TURTLE
Reptile
Indian Ocean, Indonesia,
Atlantic Ocean, Pacific Ocean

CRAB-EATING MACAQUE
Mammal
Southeast Asia

ORANGUTAN
Mammal
Indonesia,
Southeast Asia

PHILIPPINE EAGLE
Bird
Southeast Asia

BLACK-AND-RED BROADBILL
Bird
Indonesia

BAWEAN DEER
Mammal
Indonesia

MALAY TAPIR
Mammal
Indonesia,
Southeast Asia

BLUE-SPOTTED SPINEFOOT
Fish
Indian Ocean

COLETO
Bird
Southeast Asia

SOUTHERN CASSOWARY
Bird
Australia, Indonesia

LONGSPINE SQUIRRELFISH
Fish
Indian Ocean, Pacific
Ocean, Red Sea

PROBOSCIS MONKEY
Mammal
Southeast Asia
▲▲

BICOLOR DOTTYBACK
Fish
Indian Ocean,
Pacific Ocean
●

BLUE TANG
Fish
Indian Ocean,
Pacific Ocean
●

NAPOLEON FISH
Fish
Indian Ocean, Pacific Ocean
▲▲

**YELLOW LONGNOSE
BUTTERFLYFISH**
Fish
Indian Ocean, Pacific Ocean
●

PURPLE KINGFISHER
Bird
Asia, Indonesia
●

**ASIAN FAIRY-
BLUEBIRD**
Bird
Asia, Indonesia
●

Australia

TASMANIAN DEVIL
Mammal
Tasmania
▲▲

KOALA
Mammal
Australia
▲

INLAND TAIPAN
Reptile
Australia
○

EMU
Bird
Australia
●

COMMON WOMBAT
Mammal
Australia, Tasmania
●

DINGO
Mammal
Australia
○

SUPERB FAIRY-WREN
Bird
Australia
●

**EASTERN GREY
KANGAROO**
Mammal
Australia
●

THORNY DEVIL
Reptile
Australia
○

**AUSTRALIAN
BLACK WIDOW**
Arachnid
Asia, Australia
○

KOOKABURRA
Bird
Australia
●

YELLOW-CRESTED COCKATOO
Bird
Australia, Indonesia,
New Zealand
●

**GREY-HEADED
FLYING FOX**
Mammal
Australia
▲

SHORT-BEAKED ECHIDNA
Mammal
Australia
●

In the
Oceans

OPAH
Fish
Atlantic Ocean, Indian
Ocean, Pacific Ocean
▲

LEOPARD RAY
Fish
Atlantic Ocean, Indian
Ocean, Pacific Ocean
■

**SHORT-BEAKED COMMON
DOLPHIN**
Mammal
Atlantic Ocean, Pacific Ocean
●

GREAT WHITE SHARK
Fish
Atlantic Ocean, Indian
Ocean, Pacific Ocean
▲

STELLER SEA LION
Mammal
Pacific Ocean
■

SPERM WHALE
Mammal
Antarctic Ocean, Atlantic Ocean,
Indian Ocean, Pacific Ocean
▲

RED-LEGGED KITTIWAKE
Bird
North Pacific Ocean
▲

BARRACUDA
Fish
Atlantic Ocean, Indian
Ocean, Pacific Ocean
●

SOUTHERN BLUEFIN TUNA
Fish
Atlantic Ocean, Indian
Ocean, Pacific Ocean
▲▲▲

ORCA
Mammal
Antarctic Ocean, Arctic Ocean, Atlantic
Ocean, Indian Ocean, Pacific Ocean
○

HERRING
Fish
Atlantic Ocean
●

BLACK-LEGGED KITTIWAKE
Bird
Arctic Ocean, Atlantic
Ocean, acific Ocean

SWORDFISH
Fish
Atlantic Ocean, Indian
Ocean, Pacific Ocean

On the Arctic Ice Floes

RAZORBILL
Bird
Arctic regions, Asia,
Europe, North America

ARCTIC HARE
Mammal
Arctic regions

SNOWY OWL
Bird
Arctic regions

WALRUS
Mammal
Arctic regions

NARWHAL
Mammal
Arctic regions

BLUE WHALE
Mammal
Antarctic and Arctic
regions

ARCTIC WOLF
Mammal
Arctic regions

LITTLE AUK
Bird
Arctic regions,
Europe, North America

ERMINE
Mammal
Arctic regions,
Europe

BLACK-THROATED LOON
Bird
Arctic regions, Asia,
Europe, North America

POLAR BEAR
Mammal
Arctic regions

COMMON MURRE
Bird
Arctic regions, Europe,
North America

BELUGA WHALE
Mammal
Arctic regions

SPOTTED SEAL
Mammals
Arctic regions

HOODED SEAL
Mammal
Arctic regions

CARIBOU
Mammal
Arctic regions

COMMON EIDER
Bird
Arctic regions, Europe,
North America

ANTARCTIC TERN
Bird
Australia, Europe, South
Africa, South America

Tundra

LYNX
Mammal
Arctic regions, Asia,
Europe

EURASIAN BEAVER
Mammal
Asia, Europe

BROWN BEAR
Mammal
Arctic regions, Europe,
North America

RAVEN
Bird
Africa, Arctic regions, Asia,
Europe, North America

OSPREY
Bird
Africa, Americas, Arctic regions,
Asia, Europe, Indonesia

GREAT SPOTTED WOODPECKER
Bird
Arctic regions, Asia, Europe, North America

SNOW BUNTING
Bird
Arctic regions, Asia, Europe, North America

ATLANTIC SALMON
Fish
Arctic regions, Europe, North America

MOOSE
Mammal
Arctic regions, North America

MUSKOX
Mammal
Arctic regions, Europe

SIBERIAN WOLF
Mammal
Arctic regions

LEMMING
Mammal
Arctic regions

WOLVERINE
Mammal
Arctic regions, Europe

TUNDRA SWAN
Bird
Arctic regions, Asia, Europe, North America

On the Edge of the Forest

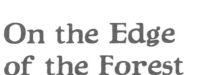

AMERICAN BLACK BEAR
Mammal
North America

ZANDER
Fish
Europe

EUROPEAN STURGEON
Fish
Europe

PORCUPINE
Mammal
North America

STUDFISH
Fish
Europe

RED SQUIRREL
Mammal
Asia, Europe

EURASIAN GREEN WOODPECKER
Bird
Europe, Middle East

SKUNK
Mammal
North America

REEVES'S PHEASANT
Bird
Asia, Europe
GREAT EGRET

Bird
Africa, Americas, Asia, Europe, Oceania
FIRE SALAMANDER

Amphibian
Europe
GREAT HORNED

OWL
Bird
Americas, Asia, Europe

EUROPEAN HARE
Mammal
Asia, Europe, Middle East

COMMON BREAM
Fish
Europe

VOLE
Mammal
Europe, North America

RED DEER
Mammal
Asia, Europe, North Africa, North America

COMMON TOAD
Amphibian
Europe

RACCOON
Mammal
Europe, North America

ROE DEER
Mammal
Asia, Europe